DATE DUE

OCT 2 6 2001			
SEP 0 4 2002			
JAN 2 7 2003			
FEB 0 7 2004			
JAN 1 1 2005			
MAR 1 5 2006			
NOV 1 5 2016			
FEB 0 1 2017			
AUG 3 1 2017			
OCT 1 9 2018			

GAYLORD   PRINTED IN U.S.A

Martha's New Daddy

Danielle Steel

Martha's New Daddy

Illustrated by Jacqueline Rogers

Delacorte Press

Published by
Delacorte Press
Bantam Doubleday Dell Publishing Group, Inc.
666 Fifth Avenue
New York, New York 10103

Library of Congress Cataloging in Publication Data

Steel, Danielle.
    Martha's new daddy / by Danielle Steel; illustrated by Jacqueline Rogers.
        p.   cm.
    Summary: Five-year-old Martha is troubled by her mother's impending marriage, but talking things over with her understanding father helps her to view the situation with enthusiasm after all.
    ISBN 0-385-29799-8
    [1. Remarriage—Fiction.   2. Divorce—Fiction.]   I. Rogers, Jacqueline, ill.   II. Title.
PZ7.S8143Man   1989
[E]—dc19   88-35253
                                                            CIP
                                                            AC

designed by Judith Neuman-Cantor

Manufactured in the United States of America
November 1989

10 9 8 7 6 5 4 3 2 1

To Nicky, wonderful, remarkable, special boy,
heart of my heart and Daddy's.

With all my love,
Mommy

This is Martha. She lives in San
Francisco. She is five years old.

Her parents are divorced. That means that her Mommy and Daddy aren't married anymore, even though they used to be. They still talk to each other on the phone. They both go to Martha's school to see the Christmas pageant or the school play, but they don't live together anymore. They got divorced when Martha was three years old.

Every Wednesday after work, Martha's
Daddy picks her up, and takes her to his
house on Telegraph Hill. He makes dinner
and she spends the night. Every other
weekend, Martha stays at her Daddy's
house again. They go for long walks in
the park, they go to boat shows and dog

shows, and the zoo, and movies. Sometimes they go to Carmel or Disneyland or San Diego. And once they even went skiing in Squaw Valley. Weekends with her Daddy are very special to Martha. That's because her Daddy is a very special person, and Martha loves him very much.

She loves her Mommy too. Sometimes it makes her sad that her Mommy and Daddy can't be together anymore. Sometimes she likes to pretend that they'll get married again, and she will be at their wedding.

One day, when Martha came home from
school, her Mommy told her that she had
a surprise. Her Mommy's friend John was
there. He came to visit a lot. He was
always very nice to Martha. Sometimes he
took her out for ice cream. Other times he

went to the beach with Martha and her Mommy. On weekends he liked to take Martha and her Mommy out for dinner. Martha's Mommy said that John was divorced too, but he didn't have any children.

Martha wondered what the surprise was. Her Mommy and John looked at each other as though it was something important.

"John and I are going to get married," Martha's Mommy said.

For a minute Martha just stared at them. She wanted to be happy for them, but she wasn't. All she could think of was her own Daddy. Now her Mommy and Daddy would never get married again. And she would never be at their wedding.

"We want you to be our flower girl," Martha's Mommy said happily.

"Where are we going to live?" Martha asked sadly.

"Right here. And next year, we'll get a new house. But for now, we'll stay here." John was moving into the house where her real Daddy had lived with them, on Russian Hill, the house where she still lived with her Mommy. But Martha knew that John would never really be her Daddy.

"What do you think, Martha?" John was smiling down at her. He gently touched her hand and then put an arm around her shoulders. It wasn't that she didn't like him. She did. But she still wanted her Mommy to go back to her Daddy.

That night, after John took them out for
dinner, Martha went to her room. When
she went to bed, she lay in the dark for
a long time, and thought about her Daddy.

On Wednesday, when her Daddy picked her up after school, Martha was very, very quiet. He asked her what was wrong. Finally, with sad eyes, Martha told him.

"Mommy is getting married."

"I know," he said quietly. "She called and told me." But he didn't look sad. He was smiling. "I think that's wonderful for her. John is a very nice man."

"You do?" Martha looked surprised.

"I do. And I hope they'll be very, very happy."

Tears filled Martha's eyes. No one understood what she was feeling. Not even her Daddy. "But that means you and Mommy will never get married again," Martha said sadly.

"That's right." Her Daddy nodded. "We won't. But we wouldn't have anyway." He looked serious now. "When your Mommy and I got married a long time ago we

loved each other very, very much. And I still love your Mommy because she's my friend and she was my wife, and she's your Mommy. But we didn't make each other happy when we were married. We don't like to do the same things, or go to the same places, or be with the same people. We just don't want to be married to each other, Martha. But one day, I might like to be married to someone else. And I think your Mommy will be very happy with John and we should be very happy for her."

Martha nodded her head slowly as she listened. It wasn't easy hearing her Daddy say that her parents didn't want to be married to each other anymore. And that they would never marry each other again. But it hadn't been easy when they got divorced either. Back then, they used to fight a lot. Her Mommy had cried a lot of the time. But that was a long time ago. Martha had always thought that if they got married again, it would be different.

"Do you really mean you would never marry Mommy again?"

"I really mean I never would. It took us a long time to get to be friends, and I wouldn't do anything to spoil that. She's a very special person to me. I'd much rather be her friend than her husband."

Martha nodded again. She was beginning to understand now.

That night, she and her Daddy went out
for pizza.

"What if John asks me to call him
Daddy?" Martha was still a little worried.

"I don't think he will. What do you call
him now?"

"John."

"I'm sure he won't change that." Her
Daddy smiled at her.

"And what if they have a baby?"

Her Daddy nodded thoughtfully. "They

might. And I might get married and have more children too. But that wouldn't make us love you less. You're our special, special little girl, and you always will be."

"And a year from now, we're going to move to a new house," Martha said, still sounding worried.

"A year is a long time from now, and a new house can be very exciting."

There was so much to think about now.

Martha was confused, but she felt better the next day when she went home. John was at the house with her Mommy. They were talking about the wedding. And Martha's Grandma was going to come from New York on a big airplane. After the wedding, her Mommy and John were going on a honeymoon to Hawaii.

"How long will you be gone?" Martha asked worriedly.

"About two weeks." John smiled as he answered.

"Oh." Martha was very quiet as she looked up at him. John sat down and put her on his lap.

"We're hoping that you would come with us."

"You were?" Martha got very excited. "To Hawaii? Can I swim there?"

"Of course you can," John said. "We'll build sand castles, and go sailing, and do lots of exciting things." Martha jumped up and down.

The wedding was in June, and it was beautiful. Martha's Mommy wore a white dress and a white hat. Martha wore a beautiful new white dress too. She had white flowers in her hair, and she carried a little bouquet of tiny white roses.

Afterward, there was a party for all their friends and relatives, and Martha's Grandma from New York was there.

The next day, John and Martha and her Mommy flew to Hawaii on a big airplane. They spent two weeks there. They had a wonderful time, finding seashells, and swimming and building sand castles on the beach. And as they flew back to San Francisco, Martha was excited about seeing her Daddy. She knew how lucky she was now, because she had three important people in her life. She had Mommy, and John.

And even though her Mommy was
married again, she knew she would always
have her very, very special Daddy.